A New True Book

RABBITS AND HARES

By Emilie U. Lepthien

CHILDRENS PRESS®

CHICAGO

White-tailed jackrabbit

Project Editor: Fran Dyra
Design: Margrit Fiddle

PHOTO CREDITS

Animals Animals—© Robert Maier, 7 (right);
© Press-Tige Pictures Oxford Scientific
Films, 13 (left), 25; © Leonard Lee Rue III,
16; © Stouffer Prod. Ltd., 17; © Oxford
Scientific Films, 21; Geo. F. Godfrey, 35;
© Mella Panzella, 39

© AP/Wide World Photos—37

The Bettmann Archive—43 (left), 44 (right)

Alan & Sandy Carey—Cover, 18, 27 (left),
32 (right)

Dembinsky Photo Associates—© Rod
Planck, 2, 11; © Sharon Cummings, 13
(right); © Dominique Braud, 29

© Jerry Hennen, 22

Photri—© Kahle, 27 (right); © Lani Novak
Howe, 43 (right)

Root Resources—© Gail Nachel, 6 (left);
© Charles G. Summers, Jr., 7 (left)

Tony Stone Images—45; © Bill Ivy, 9;
© Leonard Lee Rue III, 26; © Gay
Bumgarner, 38

SuperStock International, Inc.—44 (left);
© Roderick Chen, Cover Inset

UPI/Bettmann—40

Valan—© Herman H. Giethoorn, 6 (right);
© Aubrey Lang, 10; © Michel Bourque, 12,
31 (right); © Stephen J. Krasemann,
31 (left) 39 (inset); © Maslowski, 36

Visuals Unlimited—© Leonard Lee Rue III,
5; © William J. Weber, 14; © Glenn Oliver,
19; © Barbara Gerlach, 32 (left)

COVER: Snowshoe hare in spring
COVER INSET: Domestic white bunnies

Library of Congress Cataloging-in-Publication Data

Lepthien, Emilie U. (Emilie Utteg)
   Rabbits and hares / by Emilie U. Lepthien.
      p.   cm.—(A New true book)
   Includes index.
   ISBN 0-516-01058-1
   1. Rabbits—Juvenile literature. 2. Hares—Juvenile
literature. [1. Rabbits. 2. Hares.] I. Title.
QL737.L32L45   1994
599.32'2—dc20   93-33514
                                              CIP
                                              AC

TABLE OF CONTENTS

RABBITS AND HARES

We see rabbits so often that we don't think of them as wild animals. We watch them hop across our yards. They stop and wait, perfectly still. Their large ears pick up any sound of danger. Their sharp, bright eyes catch any movement. Their twitching nose sniffs out any unusual scent. Then they hop away.

Cottontail rabbits are active during the winter. They leave their burrows to look for food.

Rabbits and hares are mammals. Mammals are warm-blooded animals that nurse their babies with mother's milk.

There are about forty species of rabbits and

Many kinds of European rabbits are kept as pets, such as the French lop-eared rabbit (left) and the Dutch rabbit (right).

hares. Almost half of the species live in North America. Rabbits and hares live in Europe, Asia, and Africa. Today they are also found in South America, Australia, and New Zealand.

The black-tailed jackrabbit of the western United States (left) and the European hare (below)

In North America, rabbits and hares live from the far north down to the Gulf of Mexico. They are found in deserts, marshes, swamps, and forests. Rabbits like shrubs and tall grass. Hares prefer open fields.

7

SEEING, HEARING, AND SMELLING

Rabbits and hares have a good sense of smell. They twitch their nose when they are smelling. Their hearing is sharp. They can hear even the faintest sounds. Their large ears can turn one at a time or together.

Their eyesight is keen. Their big, round eyes are

The Cape hare lives in the southern parts of Africa.

on the sides of their heads. They can see behind them and to the side, but they cannot see so well straight ahead.

Rabbits keep their thick fur in good condition by licking it.

SPECIAL COATS

Rabbits and hares have thick, soft underfur. Longer, heavier guard hairs cover the underfur. They keep the animals warm in cold weather.

The coloring of rabbits and hares helps them to hide from enemies. Can you see the white-tailed jackrabbit sitting outside its burrow?

Guard hairs are brownish or grayish in color. This coloring protects the animals when they are in open fields. They cannot be seen easily when they are motionless. The color of the fur on their undersides is much lighter.

The cottontail rabbit's fluffy white tail looks like a ball of cotton.

RABBITS

Rabbits are furry animals with short, fluffy tails. They measure from 8 to 14 inches (20 to 36 cm) long. They may weigh from 2 to 5 pounds (0.9 to 2.3 kg).

Their fluffy tail is about 2 inches (5 cm) long. The tail fur is lighter underneath than on top. Cottontail rabbits were named for their fluffy white tail.

Rabbits are herbivorous, which means they only eat plants. In spring and summer they eat grasses, clover, and sometimes the sprouts of vegetables in a farmer's field.

Rabbits come out in the evening to feed on grasses (below left) and other small green plants.

Young cottontails feasting on an apple

Since rabbits do not hibernate, or sleep through the winter, they must find food in the cold months. They eat twigs and bark. They may also find fruits and berries left on trees and bushes.

PREDATORS

In the wild, rabbits live for little more than a year. Humans are their worst enemy. Millions of rabbits are killed each year for sport, food, and their fur. Many are also killed by cars on highways.

This red fox has killed a rabbit for food.

In the wild, coyotes, foxes, minks, weasels, hawks, and owls are their natural enemies.

Rabbits can travel 18 miles (29 km) per hour

when trying to escape an enemy. Frightened rabbits may leap and zigzag, but they soon grow tired. Then they try to hide in a burrow or a clump of shrubs.

A bobcat chases a snowshoe rabbit.

Baby cottontails in their grassy nest

HOMES AND BABIES

Cottontails make grassy nests where they can hide under a blanket of grass.

Most rabbits live in a den, or burrow. Sometimes they move into another

The entrance to a rabbits' den. In winter, the rabbits are snug and warm inside their underground home.

animal's empty burrow. They keep their burrows very clean and dig them close to each other. Rabbits like to live close to neighbors. Sometimes many burrows are connected in a community called a warren.

When a female rabbit, or doe, is only a few months old, she can mate with a male, or buck. Baby rabbits are called kits or kittens. They are born about a month after the doe has mated. The doe is ready to mate again as soon as they are born.

A buck may mate with several does. They all live

Rabbits dig narrow tunnels to connect the many burrows in a warren.

in burrows in the same warren. The buck guards them. He marks his territory with a scent from under his chin.

In one year, a doe may have three to five litters. There may be from two to seven kits in a litter.

Newborn rabbits cannot

This newborn baby rabbit is blind and helpless. But it will grow very quickly drinking its mother's rich milk.

see or hear. They have no fur. They are completely helpless. The doe feeds her kits very rich milk once a day. The rest of the time she leaves them alone in the burrow.

HARES

Hares are larger than rabbits. They have longer ears and legs.

Male hares are often called jacks. Females may be called jills. Their babies, called leverets, are born six weeks after mating.

Hares make shallow nests called forms in open fields. The babies are born in these nests.

At birth, the babies are covered with fur, and their eyes are open. They can hop around in a very short time.

When her babies are three days old, the mother hare takes each one to its own nest. She covers each baby with grass to hide it. She visits each baby every day, and feeds it.

Brown hare babies in their nest

At dusk, the babies gather in one place and the mother feeds each one again. Then they hop back to their own forms.

ARCTIC HARES AND RABBITS

Snowshoe rabbit changing color from winter white to summer brown

Snowshoe rabbits are really hares. In summer, their coats are dark brown. In winter, the tips of the long hairs are white. This makes them hard to see in the snow. Their feet are very large and long-furred

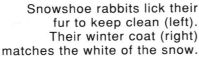

Snowshoe rabbits lick their
fur to keep clean (left).
Their winter coat (right)
matches the white of the snow.

so they can travel over
heavy snow.

Snowshoe rabbits take
good care of their fur. After
a dust bath they comb
their fur with the claws
on their hind feet. They
wash their face like a cat.
Then they lick each paw.

In North America, arctic hares live on the tundra, north of the tree line. In very cold climates, their fur is entirely white in winter.

When faced by an enemy, hares leap away. Their strong hind legs can carry them 12 feet (4 meters) with each leap. They warn other hares of danger by thumping on the ground with their hind feet.

The arctic hare is nearly three times as big as the snowshoe rabbit.

RABBITS AND RODENTS

Rabbits and hares belong to a group of animals called lagomorphs. But for many years people thought rabbits and hares were rodents. Rodents and lagomorphs are plant eaters. They are alike in many ways, but there are also many differences.

Like rodents, rabbits and hares have large front teeth called incisors. Rabbits have four upper

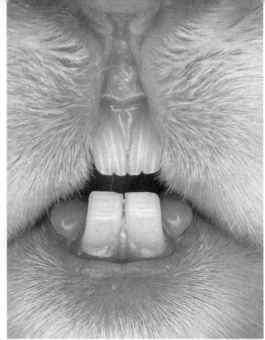

The teeth of rodents such as the beaver (left) and the rabbit (right) look similar, but the rabbit has two extra incisors on top.

incisors. Two smaller incisors lie behind the larger pair. Rodents have only two incisors in their upper jaw.

Both rabbits and rodents have two incisors in the front of their lower jaws.

Both rabbits and hares have deeply slit upper lips. Even when their mouths are closed, you can see their long front teeth.

These teeth are very sharp. They can rip up grass and twigs. They

Rabbits and hares have very strong teeth. They can chew on the tough twigs of shrubs and trees.

continue to grow throughout the animal's lifetime.

Rabbits and rodents also have grinding teeth called molars. Sometimes they are called "cheek teeth."

There is a space between the incisors and the cheek teeth. They can keep food in this space while they are nibbling on grass.

When rodents chew, they grind their food with a back and forth movement. Rabbits and hares chew from side to side.

MOST ACTIVE TIMES

Rabbits and hares are most active in early morning and at dusk. They may stay up all night eating and playing. They can also be seen in the daytime. Rabbits do not travel far from their burrows. Hares move farther from their nests.

LEGS AND FEET

Rabbits have five toes on their front feet and four toes on their hind feet. Each toe has a very sharp claw. The front claws are used for digging. Their feet have soft, hairy soles that help rabbits move over slippery places.

A rabbit's long front claws are used for digging burrows.

Rabbits do not run like other mammals. They bound along in a series of short leaps.

Rabbits and hares have long and strong hind legs. They cannot run as other animals do. Instead, they hop or leap. Their front legs help them keep their balance.

CONTROLLING THE POPULATION

Farmers and ranchers everywhere work to control the rabbit and hare population. This is especially true in North America, where there are many different kinds of rabbits and hares.

These hares were rounded up by farmers in Idaho because they were destroying crops.

A baby cottontail rabbit rests under a
tomato plant in a suburban garden.

As more land is taken
over by humans, there is
less land where rabbits
find their natural food. So
they eat farmers' crops.
The black-tailed jackrabbit,

for example, eats the early growth of wheat and corn. Other rabbits find other crops tasty. They will even eat the plants in a flower garden.

A cottontail munches on garden flowers and a black-tailed jackrabbit (inset) enjoys wildflowers in California.

Rabbits gather to drink at a waterhole in
the dry outback country of Australia.

Rabbits were taken to Australia, New Zealand, and South America. At first, rabbit meat and fur were important businesses in Australia. But rabbits soon became a problem. Because they had no natural enemies, the rabbits multiplied rapidly. They ate the grass that the sheep needed, and the sheep starved.

Around the world, farmers hunt rabbits and hares. They sink fences into the ground to keep rabbits away from their fields. They use nets to trap rabbits when they leave their burrows. They have even introduced a disease that kills rabbits and hares. So far, no method has been very successful.

RABBIT STORIES

Many stories have been written about rabbits and hares. The oldest is *Aesop's Fables*. The most famous is Beatrix Potter's *The Tale of Peter Rabbit*.

In Aesop's fable of the tortoise and the hare (below), the slow tortoise beats the hare in a race. Children love the rabbit stories and drawings of Beatrix Potter (right).

In *Alice's Adventures in Wonderland,* Alice drinks tea with
the Mad Hatter, the Dormouse, and the March Hare (left), while the
White Rabbit (right) worries about being late.

*Alice's Adventures in
Wonderland* and the Uncle
Remus stories are popular

everywhere.

And so are rabbits!
They may be the farmer's
foe, but they are still one
of our favorite furry friends.

WORDS YOU SHOULD KNOW

arctic (ARK • tik) – the cold regions of the earth around the North
    Pole

burrow (BER • oh) – a hole, or tunnel, in the ground

enemy (EN • ih • mee) – a person or an animal that tries to harm
    other people or animals

guard hairs (GARD HAIRZ) – long hairs in the outer fur of animals

herbivorous (her • BIH • ver • uss) – eating only plants, not meat

hibernate (HY • ber • nait) – to sleep through the winter

incisors (in • SIZE • erz) – long, sharp front teeth

lagomorphs (LAG • uh • morfs) – a group of animals that includes
    rabbits, hares, and pikas

leveret (LEV • er • et) – a baby hare

litter (LIT • er) – a group of baby animals all born at the same time to
    the same mother

mammal (MAM • il) – one of a group of warm-blooded animals that
    have hair and nurse their young with milk

molars (MO • lerz) – broad, flat back teeth

population (pah • pyoo • LAY • shun) – the total number of animals of
    the same kind living at the same time

rodent (ROH • dint) – an animal that has long, sharp front teeth for
    gnawing

species (SPEE • sheez) – a group of related plants or animals that
    are able to interbreed

territory (TAIR • ih • tor • ee) – an area with definite boundaries that
    an animal lives in

tree line (TREE LYNE) – the line beyond which it is too cold for trees
    to grow

tundra (TUN • dra) – a cold, treeless area where the vegetation
    consists of short grasses, mosses, and lichens

warren (WAWR • in) – a connecting series of underground burrows

INDEX

About the Author

Emilie U. Lepthien received her BA and MS degrees and certificate in school administration from Northwestern University. She taught upper-grade science and social studies, wrote and narrated science programs for the Chicago Public Schools' station WBEZ, and was principal in Chicago, Illinois, for twenty years. She received the American Educator's Medal from Freedoms Foundation.

She is a member of Delta Kappa Gamma Society International, Chicago Principals' Association, Illinois Women's Press Association, National Federation of Press Women, and AAUW.

She has written books in the Enchantment of the World, New True Books, and America the Beautiful series.